THE PRIEST AND ME

THE PRIEST AND ME

CHARLES MOHL

To order additional copies of this book, contact:
Xlibris
1-888-795-4274
www.Xlibris.com
Orders@Xlibris.com
782476

CONTENTS

Chapter One

RAY-BEGINNING

A young man just having graduation from high school stood outside the local shoe store and his attention caught a sign in the window. The sign was particularly interesting as it offered cash for college upon release after two years service in the United States Air Force. His name was Raymond Neiman and he stood on the hot and sunny street of Louisville Kentucky while contemplating the offering. He had always as a youngster wanted to fly jets, but realized the wars were nearing an end (hopefully) and there wouldn't be time for the longer training period even if he could qualify. But he thought it would be exciting and he would be eventually flying. The wars were still raging in both the Pacific as well as the European theaters. Puzzled but thinking, he walked on to the corner café where two of his fiends from school were having a coke. He joined them and soon the discussion turned to the war and what were they going to do after graduation. One had another year of school with one year more to graduate, and the other had just graduated with Ray. They both thought they would enlist in the marines. That sort of settled that little confab. Ray went on home to talk with his aging mother. He had lost his father years ago in a fatal auto accident. She said she would worry always but agreed it was his duty to fight for his country. He ran the pro's and con's through his head all night, but on the following day found him at the recruiter's office signing for the Air Force. They had a bus leaving with a couple others on board, and which bus would pick up more enroute to Lakeland Air Force base in San Antonio Texas for basic training.

The first day they were assigned their own bunk and a locker adjacent to it. They got their orientation and how to be a good airman and soon were off to the training grounds and the fun had just begun. After about a week of classes aimed at air invasion type situations, the class was given the opportunity of selecting a duty relating to the preparation and flying a B-2 or B-29 bomber. Ray chose a flight officer as he would be the third man in the cockpit during flight. His duties would involve charting the weather...their courses...maintaining full radio contact with base or others in formation...and finally be available...with the scarce bit of pilot training...to take over a wounded or downed pilot. He actually was a bit excited...and so went the training of young Ray. Near the end of training they went aboard a bomber for short practice maneuvers. They all... whether they liked it or not...got instruction on the use of a parachute...and one forced jump. Ray enjoyed the jump. The Commands in England were loosing a lot of planes due to both damage...needed repairs...and replacements...as well as qualified personnel to fly and operate the 'mighty flying warriors'. Soon they would be graduating and most of the class were off to Eglin Air Force base in the rainy British empire now filled with many flying fields scattered about the countryside. Ray arrived and got assigned a rather communal location in the corner of a large room at headquarters, a building taken over with some additions as was his corner location. He had at least a locker which would accept a padlock and one for his duffle bag. Just like down home but his old dog Rex wasn't allowed on this trip. He soon got pretty well acclimated to both the surroundings and a few of those with mouths of blather and mostly drivel with quite a bit of partaking choice English scotch thrown in...at least they would pass it around on occasion...especially after a successful return from a fruitful bombing raid. Ray had been taught that vulgarity was no substitute for wit. And so he merely observed and listened as they also played some rather heated card games when one might have thought a branch of the Bank of London was doling out cheap 'low cost' loans and a battery of lost 'hooters girls' were supplying thirst quenching beverages. Some one or two dressed in more local on the drab side of panache remained for a concealed visit with some after the games were played...argued without council...litigated without a clear verdict...and took up a sentence of sleep. But not the two with whom clandestine arrangements had been previously sought and most certainly paid for in advance. Oh Frailty, thy name be Wobbly! So now the temporary games are over and back to readiness for the fist mission aboard 'beautiful baby' painted brightly on her fore position just under the pilots' window. This would be Ray's assigned plane. Ray's call to duty was on hold for temporary repairs as one of her engines was hit by Luftwaffe attack planes as she hobbled back to base on fire at it's port wing location. They needed all planes for the bombing runs which were a daily event. The mechanics went to work soon to make what repairs they could, but parts for the maintenance guys were hard to come by and what they could scrounge from British auto storage or retailers were as valuable as the Queen's jewels. In about five days they wheeled her out in the daylight and there she stood saying...if she was one of those bumptious, bibulous frequenters of the nightly financial games...so often...they argued...was the only game in town. They were once reminded by one of the lesser partakers in their 'games of chance' that some of the boys had mowed out and fashioned a ball diamond, requisitioned some baseball equipment, and worked out their frustrations and loneliness with a rousing game of baseball.

Now that 'beautiful baby' was deemed ready to go they scheduled her to join another squadron in the air with a massive wave of bombers heading over the channel for the hidden factories making the propelled bombs that heavily attacked London and the airstrips when they could find them. That's during Winston Churchill's (better known as Winnie) famed defense of England...vowing they would fight to the very end. The bomb shelters were full, our forces were strapped with heavy losses, and that's what 'the-battle-of-London' was all about. Meanwhile Ray sat in his seat figuring the course and advising the pilots who basically had the ship on auto pilot. They were at about 3,000 feet up trying to avoid the German fighter planes. Ray had never been a church gower but established the habit of praying to himself every time a crew went out and after they returned. Now he was praying for the crew of 'beautiful baby' and well they would need his words of hope. Their position was fairly far right of the main body of the huge force of bombers. He could faintly see the Normandy cliffs and the southern fields of France. It was getting dark and most flights were by instrument at the dark of night. They gradually encountered some fighter plane interference as they came near the first scheduled target...a railroad connection to a factory that we were supposed to hit. The resistance was primarily from ground batteries firing their air defense system. Ray's plane took a few 60 caliber rounds through their main body but no injuries. They had on board a full complement of personnel...stern gunner...port side gunner...the bombardier with his gun mounted after dropping his bombs...the bow gunner and the three officers up front. They were chassed a bit by German fighter planes....mostly just a few...and concentrated on the a larger group of planes to the west of us. With an extra prayer we made it home safely...and barely as we were flying almost out of fuel hearing the engines coughing several times telling us to get down quickly. And we did! So far Ray had been the freshman of the class but now that he passed the test of virginity, he deserved the passing of the scotch with congrats to him. Within himself he gave the credit to his faithful prayers. Perhaps God was watching. This heavy bombing strategy was between Oct. of '44 to April of '45 when it pretty much was over (May 7, 1945 when Germany made an unconditional surrender while US dropped the atomic bomb on Hiroshima and Nagasaki Aug 7, 1945 and the whole business of WWII was over. Ray's first raid was late 1944 and he was involved in the all out push on Berlin. The big raid in '45 was an amassing effort especially in putting together enough B-29 bombers with personnel and cargo to get-the-job-done. His team was ready and it would be an all night flight with the cover of darkness they hoped would discourage the Luftwaffe from attempting to stop this Armageddon. In fact it really did. Ray's position in the flight plan was far right as they flew in formation. They had a fairly easy time of the flight over as the Germans apparently were saving all they had left in fighter planes for their final defense of Berlin and what was left of their railroad systems. True to form they were waiting for our bombers and let go with all they had. The antiaircraft weapons opened up continuously and the Luftwaffe pilots who were excellently trained and experienced went after our massive fleet of attackers. It was getting light...they were getting better vision...better aim at the retreating American fleet...one could see many were hit....and suddenly 'beautiful baby' also was hit as she was well on her way back home. She was riddled with antiaircraft fire tearing into the fuselage and wounding the center gunner. A Luftwaffe plane swung in at Ray's port side and was partially out of our sight as it sprayed machine gun fire at our cockpit killing the bow gunner...and as the plane went into a circular dive...came back around.... hit the cockpit again apparently seriously wounding....or it soon appeared...killing the pilot. The co-pilot was also hit and you could see blood from his left side and shoulder as well as his head...probably from shattering broken up parts and debris off the plane...Ray was also hit and could try and cover his arms while moving as quick as he could with the plane suddenly bumping and turning as though partially out of control. The injured co pilot moved to the pilot's seat... after pushing the pilot's body from his seat...Ray took up his seat and grabbed hold of the dual controls and struggled to hold the plane up and on a straight course. He could soon see smoke coming from one of the engines causing the plane to want to veer off to the opposite direction. They were still some distance from the home base and suddenly realized they might have to attempt a crash landing or jump out and abandon ship. Ray prayed for guidance and kept holding tight to the steering controls. He tried to talk to the co pilot who now had his hands on the controls and nodded that he could hear him and was okay with handling the controls. Ray immediately got on the radio with home base for instructions and a report of their faltering situation. Base responded with instruction to hold course...they would have emergency equipment ready if a landing would occur... also navel vessels were notified and put on watch over the known route of Ray's troubled situation...should they have to ditch over the channel. Ray further reported the port wing engine now showing fire and more smoke. Should the gas in that wing catch on fire the ensuing explosion would be the end of all their careers and one might find them by a stone monument in a French cemetery with their names and rank. Ray talked with God again and prayed for his crew and a successful result of their attack on the enemy. They were loosing altitude and making it very hard to hold the damaged ship on any course but an incline. They were also very low on fuel. The ship was bucking like a wild steer in a cowboy rodeo and the injured co pilot was awake but barely able to hold the steering controls. Ray took hold and prayed again for help from both the base and the Almighty high above. Ray knew from school that since there was a patron saint for birds and fowl of the air...there must be a patron saint for flying machines. Let's hope so! It was getting worse by the minute and too late to jump with all that water below. It now appeared that Ray was in charge and could only hang on...keep in touch with base for anything anyone could do...and above all keep praying. Land was in sight and the base very near by. The right engines were sputtering and obviously running out of fuel.. all left was the strength in Ray's arms and his belief there would be courage and strength breathed into him. So the finish line was in sight...but it was obvious he wouldn't make the landing strip...missed a tree...banged over top of a hedge row and bounced off the ground turning completely around and came to rest almost on it's back. It would explode any minute...the emergency crew was right out front...Ray pushed open what was left of the pilot side window and jumped loose pulling the injured copilot with him. They fell forward toward the waiting emergency team as 'beautiful baby' went up in flames along with a huge explosion. Ray laid there for a minute with the copilot almost on top of him and gave a smile.... saying to himself....*my prayers were answered*. This experience could well put light on his eventual entering the Catholic Seminary to be ordained a priest. And so it goes. Ray was taken immediately to the aid station, the copilot and gunner still but badly wounded... were taken to the nearest hospital facility....another crew would recover the bodies of the remaining crew and that will be the finale for the life and those who relied on her. Amen.

Chapter Two

THE-SEMINARY

Ray Neiman was one of the only full time real persons in this story did as his experience and prayers while serving the US Air Force during WWII caused him to think out and undertake. He had no special education or training and felt he was perhaps saved by the faith and strength of his relationship with his piers and prayers. What has been described is what has been told to me reluctantly by Ray with whom we developed over the years into a close personal friendship. So he entered I believe form him a well known eastern seminary to become an ordained Catholic priest, He must have been when he entered at about 28 and came out with his ordination at about 31 or 32. Although I'm not actually certain and I've delved into many church records and don't find any substantive information under his full name which begins with Raymond. Upon his graduation and ordination, he apparently was assigned to a Kentucky parish in the Covington area and served for a number of years.

Chapter Three

The-New-Priest-At-Work

Forsooth - his quiet, charismatic charm captivated most all with whom he met, including me. Even when he eventually retired (or tried to). His big moment came when one day he got a call to meet with the bishop. He entered, went through the customer obsequies, and listened to the Bishop. "Father Ray", he started, "I'm taking you out of religion for a time. I've got a special project I want you to take over and develop". "Your Excellency, just what is it you want me to do?", Ray responds. Just off the record "I want you to start and develop a boys home", said the Bishop. "Well", questioned Father Ray, "How much money do I have to work with?" "None", replied his excellence, "I have 20 acres of land near Lexington for you to work with and I know of your association with the deeper pockets in this area that certainly you're the man for this assignment". The waiter brought in a fine glass of sherry for the two who chatted for a bit over the possibilities of the good this venture could blossom into. With the formalities out of the way...and no one looking...Ray shook hands and gave a quick hug to his Excellency. Now what to do thought the new ordained developer. But it wasn't long before a trust fund was established, money rolling in the Father Ray's fund, and shovels in the ground for the start of the Campbell Home for Boys. One of his principal contributors was Bill Favorite who not only put in some sizable funds but introduced Ray to a group of investors from Michigan with whom he had been a graduating member, all alumnus of the University of Michigan. Bill had been an investor and director of the fledgling enterprise and encouraged Fr. Ray to invest (funds he had supervision and authority to invest and re-invest over) and he would personally back his contribution should a question arise. More importantly Fr. Ray was brought to the group because of both his management experience and his great fund raising success. Personally he had no money nor income from the church, but with Bill's backing would gain a little and the Boys Home would do very well. Fr. Ray came to the board meeting, met the group and made his commitment. If one might wonder how Fr. Ray got along without any visible source of income. He explained to me he never had a problem for food. He could always stop at a parish house and was often invited for lunch or dine at private homes. He was true to his faith that God would take care. He had a rich uncle who kept him in transportation annually with a good used car. He never worried with his irresistible charm and smile, as he was well taken care of. Occasionally the Uncle would give him a few shares of stock, guess what, he would parley them into a gain and come out with a little spending money. He did have some income from his serving communion and his short but inspiring homilies following communion. He did well and was true to his vows of chastity and poverty. He was twice declared Man-of-the-Year for Kentucky, one being in 1973 during Governor Nunn's time in office. He was also a leader in presenting Kentucky Colonel awards to certain selected people and I was one and was please to have the commission but more coming by selection from father Ray.

In my college days and little before, I often thought about life and death and was always looking for someone with an advanced intelligence to discuss religion in general. This is where I find my match and become a full out player and take the first private opportunity for engage Fr. Ray in serious debate. After a group meeting attended by Fr. Ray, I talked with him a little at the historic White Horse Inn over a martini...a beverage of his choice and invited him to see our house, have dinner, and spend the night. His driver and sponsor had plans for the evening and would be available for their departure on the morrow. We had a silver bullet and talked over the meal. I knew I had the right debating opponent as he would be intransigent in holding to his vows. We talked about his background and that's where I got a lot of the air force information and other background matters he volunteered to talk about. He wondered a bit about my divorce, as I offered a few somewhat vague responses. I closed with a verse from Mathew *"He that troubleth his own house shall inherit the wind"*, he quickly came back with *"and the fool shall be servant to the wise of heart."* With that quick parley of wit we closed for the evening and off to the mythical realm of Morpheus.

Chapter Four

THE CRUISE

Before Bill Favorite and Fr. Ray left back for Kentucky I *was* advised of two upcoming events involving previous years of joint activities. One was the cruise to the Bahamas sponsored by the Detroit Chamber of Commerce (which for years had been a cruise around Lake Michigan with the usual activities and lectures on current events facing the business world). This year it would be to the Bahamas as the former longer trips were loosing partakers, thus this new plan. The cruise would leave mid September for four days and nights from Fort Laughterdale Florida.... indicated Bill... and the second was an invite by Fr. Ray to the Kentucky Derby at which he would supply tickets and we would obtain accommodations. Sounded like a winner to me with Fr. Ray as a partner, I could continue on our debate that begun at my house. I had cases to dispose of and a book to write (at least start) and so September came all too soon and I was looking at only a few days before the debarkation from Florida. I got in touch with Ray and he was good-to-go. I had one dress up outfit for dinner and old time sailing clothes for whatever old business hounds do for occasional fun. We left port in late afternoon to sail over night. We would have plenty of time for cocktails and dinner (which are usually super lavish). Dinner was 'out-of-sight'. They also went overboard with a huge buffet for bed lunch with fruits, goodies, and drinks of course. We were off to bed. Since it was part of the cruise package, we all opted to remain on board and take tours by boat or whatever we wanted to see on the many islands. The first day we took an organized boat sight seeing cruise around the many islands...at least the major stops...one a excellent sea food lunch at *'Fat Tuesday'* on Nassau Island. We finished the day viewing the harbor at Grand Bank Island in the bay where we were anchored. Dinner was excellent with a wine selected by Fr. Ray. It was certainly a 'blessed' group going first class chaperoned by their personal pastor. The second night we had tickets for the night club Charlie's 602 Club again on Nassau Island. We came dressed in our best and Fr. Ray had on his collar but without his black standard priestly attire. The head waiter seated us at a large oval shaped table with six chairs (aside - I wondered later whether he had something in mind). We sat, greeted the waitress, and ordered a round of martini's at Father's request except for Bill Favorite, who stuck to a Manhattan. We were about to order having given the carte du jure a thoughtful comment or two, as the head waiter approached our happy assemblage. He asked if we would mind his seating two ladies with us cautioning that they were nuns on vacation. We looked at each other and Fr. Ray and unanimously okayed his gesture. He escorted the two and introduced them as Miss Mary and Miss Meagan and seated them. We stood and greeting them to our round table (and thinking a bit of levity might relax the now larger group) said, 'Hello, this is Bill, George Bill's friend, and our personal pastor Fr. Ray who already had cautioned us to go easy on our off-color jokes", and sat down. They all chuckled and again I opened up with 'now-let-the-games-begin'. Meagan looked at me with a somewhat churlish look while Mary was a bit indifferent. They were dressed in regular, we call it civilian clothes, and had their hair done up short and conservative. They wore no outward evidence giving away the disguise of their occupation. No facial makeup but each had taken some sun, which delivered color from it's troublesome rays. We all had wine with dinner and the two ladies had a small taste. During the meal I excused my self for a moment and went to the desk and asked the waiter for a piece of paper on which I wrote *"please call"* *251-664-1973*. As dinner was coming to a close and the band was playing our songs, I gathered my wits and asked Meagan (as I stood and reached for her hand making it difficult to refuse and asked) if she would like to dance. She looked a bit surprised and first turned to her companion and then said, "sure, I'd like to". The 'boys' got a big smile as I took her hand and moved toward the center of the floor. I whispered, "so glad you accepted and it's nice to meet you, or better yet hold you", "Not so fast, your friends are watching, she said". The music was almost over and as it ended she moved away and started to walk so I reached and took her hand, turned her back and said, "just one more they're playing our song, it's *Moonlight Serenade*". She came back and I held her closely as we moved slowly to the romantic music. I whispered, "you dance well for a lady in your sheltered position". I then held her closer and gave her a small kiss under her ear and remained silent humming to the music which to my dismay stopped. I thanked her for the dance. She said nothing. We returned to our somewhat surprised audience, especially her partner, Mary. We received a light, polite clap of the hands as we returned to the table and prepared for our Pastor's brief benediction. We then got up, said our goodbyes, and as we departed each talking with one or another, I slipped the note into Meagan's hand with a parting smile. And so it was over. Maybe.....? By this time the evening was spent, we were likewise, and called for a retreat. As we headed for our room, F. Ray kidded me a little about my unabashed attention to Miss

Meagan. I replied with a weak rebuttal suggesting *'you can't blame a man for trying-no matter how stacked the odds might be against you'*. We retired, Father kneeling at his bed in prayer and me in brushing my teeth, Light's out. Forsooth and what a day? The next day we investigated one activity that was on of the selling points for the cruise, some rich entrepreneur giving us a power point lecture on his board on how to make more money. Ray and Bill dutifully attended, I went on deck, got a bloody Mary, and joined the ping pong tournament. Also shot a few basket while waiting. Maybe it was the second Bloody Mary that spelled success, no- it was pure talent I walked away with the fake trophy - or, was it poor competition? We gathered for a nice lunch on board...if you don't know for sure where to go.... you can always count on great food on a known cruise. In the afternoon we all took serious naps. Nothing like readiness for dinner. That came and went with superlative comments by unanimous vote. Ray and I adjourned to the afterdeck, took comfortable chairs and resumed a follow-up on his last retort to my quoting the Book of Mathew on inheriting the wind...not forgetting Rays crushing response, 'the fool shall be servant to the wise at heart'. I asked him if he was suggesting I being the fool and he the wise at heart? He failed to answer. Let silence speak for you when in doubt, or better the word of Thoreau 'better to remain silent and thought a fool, than open one's mouth and remove all doubt'. Neither of us would want our silence covered or judged by Thoreau's classic truth. So an impasse for the moment. This seemed an appropriate time to offer my Bill Maher 'terrific-ism' on his definition of faith...*'the purposeful suppression of critical thinking'*. That's a lot to think about especially when the dictionary defines faith as an attempt to prove that which cannot be proved. This brought the good Father to not wanting to open his mouth at the moment and merely said that this discussion on opposite sides beautifully affirms the truism that you don't have to agree with a person to leave a difficult discussion and remain friends. We are good friends and shall remain.... better get a good night's sleep and we'll look for a brighter tomorrow with renewed vigor over the validity and value of the bible. The cruise was over and we all returned to our corners in the ring of life and begun readying for the Kentucky Derby.

Fr. Ray had basically retired or tried to. With his allure he was always on call appealing to smaller parishes who would call him when they knew where he was at their time. A number of former priests and other lay people bought an 80 acre horse farm nearby and passed ownership on it from time to time. Each prior owner would own it until he sold or either developed debilitating illness requiring assisted care, or die. Then the next would buy in with little at stake financially. Ray was in the mix and his opportunity to buy in came up and he opted to become a farmer manager of the horse business. He was outstanding at the race tracks but less that a master of horsemanship. Anyway I was invited to come visit and he jokingly said we could attempt to resolve all the idiosyncrasies and wonders of the universe. A joke of course but certainly to me a well crafted dodge like a fumble of the ball on fourth down. In the meantime I hadn't gotten a call from Meagan and had to give up as I had no phone number nor address by which to try and reach her. I was watching the Rachel Maddow show with her shrilling manner presenting her eight o'clock show when the phone rang...it showed unidentified user...which I usually don't answer....but I did. The person calling identified herself as Meagan Grunewald and said, "I had thought and thought about the note but at least owed you a thank you for the dance and tried to overlook the kiss on the cheek...but why did you give me the note....You knew I was already promised to the Lord and shouldn't even be talking to you." "But you are talking to me", I said. "I can't talk any further. I'm sort of being watched. The Mother Superior called me in and questioned me as to what had caused my happier attitude and being caught singing while at work. I don't dare writing from the covenant or you can be sure it would somehow get to the Mother Superior and I'd be in bigger trouble than now." "How can we get to know each other without meeting and talking about ourselves and aspirations", I replied. "I'll give you my mothers address and you can write if you insist", she said. "Don't say that," I snapped back, "I want to get to know you and more about your background and why you're where you are". No further response but she did say, "Her is my address, write it down and I'll try to think more about what to do". She hung up. At least I have an address. I guess there would be no gain to write right back as our phone conversation was fairly clear as to the each party's feelings. If her answers were about careers or business, I loose....if her answers were from feelings, I may have won...a least a foot-in-he-door. Guess I'll let it ride for a short time and she if she does think more about us.

Chapter Five

MEAGAN-THE-PRIEST-HORSE-FARMER

In the interim between my law office, new romance, and -the upcoming Kentucky Derby, I hustled with some client phone calls and directions for my private secretary, and chose the derby. First thought I would answer Fr. Ray's invite to the horse ranch. It was a pleasant drive through the countryside checking my instructions for his new rancher's residence. Typical house with hitching post at the mail box out front. Cute...but I arrived by auto and not horseback. Ray was there to welcome and was busy creating a special multi ingredient salad. It had lettuce, tomatoes, mango, artichoke, raisins, cucumbers, shrimp, onions, celery and a few more I can neither identify nor wish to force on my stomach. I hope there's lots of dressing to kill the surprise. Sorry it was his special vinegar mix. On the subject of drinks Ray brought out a present from one of the whiskey bootleggers operating freely in nearby woods....unknown ostensibly by local enforcement. Bourbon whiskey is normally dark brown but for the Reverend...that's what they called him... they had refined it several times and presented him with quart jar of whiskey pure clear as water. He offered me a taste and it was nothing like a normal shot of good bourbon whiskey, it was smooth, no bite and very nice. I got only one shot at the basket and his generosity was ended along with exhibit A, the jar. We later sat at on the porch and renewed the (we won't call it a debate any more, just a heated discussion with no judicial decision or joint letter of understanding).

I'll start by suggesting much doctrine is preserved by the careless perpetuation of simple starters for children by their parents who never took the time to consider this to be a purposeful suppression of critical thinking. Take for example the first indoctrination from birth in the little over simplified child verse like *Jesus loves me this I know, because the bible tells me so*....makes no real sense (logic, wisdom) as no child begins to understand such concepts that still challenge and test biblical scholars in their continuing efforts to understand it all as proof of the existence and over simplification of our being. I know from my own experience when my mother put me to bed at age six and taught me a simple prayer and used language....like God, heaven, and death. I was even scarred and cried....I didn't understand...and I didn't want to die. Biblical scholars research tends to always rely on the bible as scholarly proof...when, in fact, it is just a large compilation of antediluvian (the old testament) writings and a collection of many short stories (the new testament) written or compiled 70 or 80 years after the disciples where a special group formed to follow a person, philosophy, or religion. The known twelve followed Jesus probably at that time not knowing he was adorned through symbolism..... Lord. My reading of the new testament passages indicate the most often used explanation of God are the symbolisms taken from the gatherings of the early disciples with an ordinary carpenter fellow in Jerusalem. When the scholars, preachers, others by many names fail to find objective proofs, they turn to the word 'symbolisms' (it appears accepted are the use of symbols to invest in things with a representative meaning or to represent something abstract by something concrete). Let me go back to basis/source (this is just one source) of whether there is or isn't a God, i.e. the bible. Now a collateral issue pops out it's head....who's bible? We Christians generally believe the King James version once fairly universally dubbed as 'the' work...now we have a multitude of translations that suit whoever wants it to better fit their obvious own conception of the God existence - and there are many such translations). Thus, speaking as a lawyer, when you have no object facts, nor any law but the bible as proof or law, you pound the table. (note: hardly can we all accept as 'facts', religious rules or bible stories by some one (Jesus and Mary Magdalene) who become deified via the symbolism, 'magic', and represent religious 'facts' not real facts. Thus many still regard those religious facts as concrete and real. In literature this 'magic or transformation from real to deity are called eponyms. My argument is now indeed spent and I have opened my mouth as a fool - so say some of the multitude. I've made my case and pounded the table. "Probably enough for your ears or more perhaps than enough", I said. Just a quick aside which reminds me of a light rebuke I got from one of my favorite judges who admonished me by saying, "You made your point and it was good, but before you ruin it's impact and loose the jury, for heaven sakes sit down". Having patiently listened to all of the above 'lecture' by me, Fr. Ray smiled and quietly said, "One day you will look on high, fold your hands, ask God for forgiveness, and be a better man as I have been....saved by prayer. Listening to your lawyerly presentations, you appear to have been doing your homework. Now let's pray together silently and ask good things for our friendship. Fr. Ray retired to his hand made alter and prayed while I poured me a stinger thinking about Father's words and Meagan. Forsooth.

Chapter Six

KENTUCKY DERBY

I realized I hadn't heard from or received any news from Meagan, although I had her mother's address and a mild invite to write through her. So I took pen in hand, actually with poor hand scratching ....wrote

Dear Meagan,

I've missed you and the time you sort of shared with the dance at the night club. We need to get together and dance, have dinner, or even sit in the park and hold hands and share some thoughts on what a future we might make. We won't know unless we try. Please write and tell me when we can get together even if we meet at mother's house. What does mom think of your vacationing at such a sinful place. Maybe she'll wish you the best and be on my side. Doesn't hurt to dream. Please call or write, PEACE! Love & kisses.

Back to the road to the derby and the fortunes we undoubtedly won't come close to realizing. I don't understand horses, I don't ride them, I don't talk to them, I don't even feed them apples. However, I will enjoy the company of our traveling foursome and the sweet savoring of the legendary mint juleps. Bill Favorite had the 'inns' with the motel and even though most were booked for the Derby, he managed two adjoining rooms for the 'fab' four. Speaking of the fab four the Kentucky Derby is the thing, the high point of the year in Kentucky and much as the super bowl in football or the final four in basketball back up north. There were parties before the race, parties during the race, and actually heavy parties in the inner track during the race. Of course Fr. Ray was a most distinguished member of the inner clan and we had the very best seats in the upper deck. Father of course knew his horses well but I understand from him the dog track better. Little did anyone know (except the horse) that Secretariat would win, let alone a hat trick before the season was over. As I said earlier, I knew nothing about horse racing...and cared less....and so I bet and lost two dollars on the smallest horse and the ugliest jockey....but I brought back five empty mint julep glasses complements of the derby entertainment committee. We laughed, cheered, clapped hands and did every thing but touch Secretariat who was abash with roses and a very rich jockey. Maybe the winner will invite Fr. Ray to his after race cerebration at his horse ranch complex, whoever or wherever that was. It took a while to get back to the motel as Father had one close by stop he had promised to make....probably an investor in his Boys Home which now was fully operational and letting out some young ready engineers. When we finally got back to the motel still on two feet, we were ready to crash...and we did. The next morning was Sunday and Fr. Ray was up bright and early and wanted to go to communion. So he got me awake and we left for about a 60 mile drive to the Cistercian Monastery home of the Trappist monks whose order took vows of total silence...however their choir sang beautifully....and I guess singing wouldn't be considered breaking the vows of silence....and what does it matter. Father knew all the controversial history of the monastery and the training abbey of Gethsemane nearby. Also they built a retreat house where a penitent could come and use the facilities and pay whatever they felt right about. The abbey in 2014 experienced a $1,000,000 embezzlement scandal by their accountant and others went to jail for not only theft but malicious sex scandals. Oh, well the monastery was a typical vast brick structure built in 1860 and now under bankruptcy proceedings. We arrived and had to sit high in the balcony for visitors even though Fr. Ray was dressed appropriately and recognized as a priest... but so what...we went there for communion which we took as offered by one of the monks....most were ordained. On the way back to the motel we found the old route 247 north to Berea and the original Boone Tavern, stopped for lunch and viewed the collection of artifacts. Ray being a born and bred Kentuckian was always talking about his favorite subject. We finished at the tavern and as soon back to the motel.

The next day neither having received a phone call nor a letter, I left the boys for the party route and sat down at a quiet place and wrote to my presumptive and hopefully sweetheart...although certainly no poof of any reciprocation in ardor or enthusiasm yet.....

Dearest Meagan

Since I haven't heard from you by phone, letter or carrier pigeon, I'm honestly depressed, I think of you all the time and it's bad for my work. I had hoped you would have had a girl to girl serious talk with your mother and tell her of your feelings.....if you have any for me and my wishes to get together and at least talk. You're smart and imaginative and can come up with something....a day off...sickness....vacation....you can think of one but we must get on before it's too late. I guess perhaps I don't know what real love is, but I'm having feelings I can't explain but the feelings I had dancing and holding you with alile kiss and no wanting to release you keeps coming

back night after night. One last plea or I'll have
to surrender, but I have no history of being a
looser, I love you and pleases come through with
a message. Love & kisses.

I was dozing a bit as I finished the letter and walked
back to see what was going on with the boys. They weren't
back yet from whatever escapade had caught their fancy...
likely a festive party with an ambush of mint juleps to
sooth their feelings from loosing whatever they bet but not
on the winner, Bill Favorite. And his friend departed until
a further meeting of consequence developed, I held Father
back for a short time and confessed my more than a little
interest in one of his nuns...of course the one he met and
watched our dance...and about which he made some sly
comment to me at the Bahama motel. "I think I know you
pretty well and also that you're a ladies man....no harm or
judgment intended", He offered, "And I knew and thought
very highly of your former wife....and as you more than
anyone appreciates, I'm sworn to the tenets of the church
and the ethical rules of confidentiality. I also don't know
Miss Meagan and what she thinks about the situation. After
all she's bound by the same vows, ethics and the rules we
both live by. I really don't know what to say or what it is
you expect me to say. In truth, I sort of feel for you both.
I will say finally this much and you know that the church

doesn't really understand my very charismatic approach to religion and my homilies....but the Bishop silently in truth approves...and so for you two in the end I think you will use good judgment and find an answer. I went to my office and put in a call.

Chapter Seven

Meagan-Troubles-Convent

I took up the phone and put in the call which was answered by an elderly lady that said she was Meagan's mother and was directed to notify you of her situation. "Good heavens, I said, what on earth has happened". "She's in the hospital with a nervous break down and I hope doing better and hope ready to be discharged and come home. All she keeps saying is 'just one more dance, please just one more, I'll tell the band'. Then she talks about you as I guess you are the one that she's talking about. "Can I see her right away, I'm not far in Flint"? "The doctor says no visitors and get plenty of rest", she said. "I'm the person she's talking about, I'm in love with her and must see her". Hasn't she talked to you about our meeting and the few letters and a call, and now this, Has she been out of the convent long"?, I said. "The convent is most upset over all this business with you and are not sure what discipline will be sought by the

Mother Superior here at the convent. This is an unusual case and even we don't know what to do. Her father pulled strings to get her in and now this," she replied. "She acts like a different person since she and her friend Sister Mary went on that cruise to the Bahamas." "you haven't answered my question on what you think", I demanded. "We don't know. At first we discouraged the talk and later we just didn't know. She's our only child and we want the best for her but we thought the solid work as a nun would fulfill both her wishes and ours. All in all we want her to be happy", she took out a hanky to wipe her sudden tears. I decided to see her and asked what hospital she was in and how would I get there. "It's Mercy Hospital and they won't be glad to see you", she insisted. "I'm gong right down there and I'll see you folks later." I had made the call in late morning and was now on my way down I-75 for the Hospital and thinking of just how to work my way into the current development. I arrived, parked, and entered at the front desk and politely asked for Miss Gruenwald and was more or less rudely told she was not to have any visitors except family. "Well, I'm her brother, what room is she in". "She doesn't have a bother sir"..."then I'm her private doctor and I must see her." "I don't believe you but I'll check with the office", she said as she rose to walk away. I went to the nearest hall and was met by a nurse or another white coat and asked where I might find her room. The person said to check at the nursing desk near the rooms. I approached the desk and saw a person being pushed in a wheelchair looking suspiciously like who I thought it might be. I approached quickly, stopped the person operating the mobile chair, and low-and-behold, it appeared to be Meagan. Her hair had grown out a good deal and was messed up a bit and she looked a bit pale, and at first didn't seem to recognize me. I thought I would surprise her in case she was not totally awake and said, "Would you like to dance, they're playing 'Moonlight Serenade' and I remember the night". The nurse was stunned and taken back while Meagan started to cry and said, "Do I know you, what are you doing here"? I reached in and gave her a big hug and tried to wipe her eyes with the robe around her. The nurse still shocked indicated she must report to the station. Let's get her back to her room. I noticed it was 12. She did not leave but called the desk with her report of my entrance. The nurse then started to get her back into the bed as the recipient of the call came hustling in. Briskly she said, "who are you and what are you doing here failing to observe the no visitor sign"? "This seems a most unpleasant place and for your information I'm Sir Galahad and with my white horse have come to rescue this incarcerated maiden from her present bondage", I said. "You're not the least funny and I'll have to call security and have you removed, she retorted". "Better make sure he's pretty big guy or I'll remove him. I'm an attorney and you'll be slapped with a nice big lawsuit, simply said "I'm in love with Miss Meagan and just learned about her. Please if in your infinite wisdom we can be alone for a few minutes, I'll leave peacefully", I said. The head nurse now satisfying herself she had put out her best performance and was cooling a bit... having showed us all her authority decided to speak nicely. "I don't want any trouble just a few minutes and if you insist, I'll leave then and come back later", I offered. In that same infinite wisdom and perhaps one who had been in love herself at one time, calmed a bit more and gave her assent to my having that few minutes but not without a witness. I moved the chair and looked her in the teary face and spoke, "Honey, what in the world is going on with hospital business and the people being so difficult"? She was still shook and chokingly said, "I was talking about you and kept repeating how I wanted another dance and some of my friendly sisters were worried and got the Mother Superior informed who hustled in quickly to try and comfort my erratic conduct. They thought I should see a councilor of same type and see if they could diagnose the problem", she reached over and held her arms out for a hug and got a firm one with another kiss on the cheek. "We've got to get you out of here. What is your standing or situation with the convent, and more importantly what do you want to happen".? "I just don't know. I think about all the time, but with the family and my vows to the church, I'm not only terribly confused but thinking and having bad dreams when I wake up shouting expressing my feelings and not knowing where I am, or sometimes who I am before they quiet me down, and talk calmly until I come to be aware of what's happening". "I don't think you have to loose it all or pick only one action and loose the rest. Leaving the cloister doesn't prohibit your praying and loving God. There is always a basis for compromise unless by chance the Church takes the arbitrary position that it's us or being expelled or some other action". "My thinking is difficult as I remember your last letter when you talked about not knowing or understanding real love but that your heart seemed to sound differently. Now remembering our dancing together and the feelings I felt that night makes me feel the same. I feel like I'm falling in love and you make me feel this way." 'It would seem we are in agreement on the subject of our feelings and I vote that we figure out a way to get you out of here and deal with your unstable and emotional situation by perhaps as your friends suggest. Then when the time is right...we can talk together on the plan which I've been more anxious to settle and which I hope can be reasonably soon. 'I said. "First I'll speak with the nurse and the doctor or whoever that might be and see what they have in mind. I can talk with the Mother Superior and see if she will tell me what she is about to do or what she recommends for Meagan. That would help if she takes you back in for at least temporary time. Also there is the possibility you could live back temporarily at your folks until I get my office affairs in order. She was tired and weary and so I smiled and gave her another kiss on the cheek as she turned to rest. I left with a basket full of unsolved catch-22s and about to make an appointment with the Mother Superior soon. The social worker sought and recommended a physiologist who interviewed her and recommended a rehabilitation facility she knew about and highly recommended. While Meagan seemed to be adjusting to the pressures and stress on her, this move would help unreel the basket full of competing stressful situations weighting heavily on her mind. He Mother Superior finally felt it was in her best interest and released her from the hospital to be admitted the *Good Fellows Rehabilitation Center.* I was the only visitor allowed in for the 28 days in an effort the cut down on the competing pressures. I let her rest for a couple days so she could acclimate with both the surroundings, the personnel and the routine activities. This also gave me some time to get back into the office and get some work done. I had a kind of difficult labor relations problem with the employees who were wanting to join the AFL union. So I met with their individual groups explaining the benefits they already had and more promised by their new employer. I stressed that the business was new and had to get it's legs and walk before it could run in the big time. You don't shy away and be threatened by their demands. We fired a couple unruly workers and hired a few more well picked as we could in short time. The election was coming up and I hadn't seen my sweetie yet. And so it goes in what the some observers joke as members of the swamp. And - who would want to attempt cleaning it out. How did I get off the track with by negotiating with local people.

Got in my car and drove to Good Fellows to see her. She was sitting out on a tile over concrete area facing a flower garden and some ceramic objects placed in and near the walk around garden. There were a couple others sitting alone and nearby but out of our hearing range. She smiled as I approached, pulled up a chair and gave her a hug. I asked how she was doing and how things were progressing with the treatment here at Good Fellows. She felt her private meting with a psychologist and better yet group meetings we interesting and helpful. "But honey, I do miss you and need to get you out and so you get a feel for what's going on out there that I has been missing while cloistered up at the convent", she said. "You look good, but always did to me, I do hope you are able to deal with the stress as you meet with others who obviously have similar pressures nagging at them, I have a big union election coming next week and I have a good deal of preparation for it as well as other clients 'chomping-at-the-bit' to complete their matters. I think it will be better for both of us while you get your self feeling better over it all while I get things back in order at the office. We'll be apart for about a week but it can serve us well', I offered. I love you and maybe we can leave here soon, take a little vacation so you can see what crazy things are going out there. We have cars out there running without a driver, massive malls and shopping centers galore, and always traffic jams, accidents, texting while driving and 'much-much-more' as they say in TV commercial. Forsooth once again and so it goes and did go until I received a call from Good Fellows medical and social director that Meagan was doing well and talking nothing but joining with you on a trip out in the crazy world. I needed to get back and deal with the election coming so I'll have to leave for short time. I drove to the company office and also talked with those at the election site and talked again with the co-counsel and management team who seemed to think the outcome would be favorable for the company. I wished the team the best and parted.

Chapter Eight

VACATION-FREE-FINAL-VERSE

And now back to pack for a little trip and who knows what's in store for the near future. I'm driving the touring Mazda and will pack up tomorrow for the big venture in my future also. So let's try and move that mystical rock over the mountain as Sisyphus just missed, but my rocks are a little smaller and believe me will make it over the bar. Remember that he was a mythical creature and I'm for real and in real love. During the break period Meagan's folks visited her and brought her some traveling clothes, personals and whatever it is women carry....and social media reports it could be a lot. In the meantime I had secured tickets and the best suite on the top deck and overlooking the ocean. It was a long drive to make it so I arrived early after a call for the change and left early on Thursday and we would get on the cruise ship early on Friday for the trip to Nassau. We lucked out and traffic wasn't too bad. I had hoped she maybe could drive, but she said she did drive earlier but wasn't up to try it now and maybe spoil everything. We boarded got our pictures taken with the Captain and went through the lines leaving our passports, tickets and getting the luggage sent to the suite. We were met by a short Port a Rican Steward. He was all smiles and expressed such an accommodating personality that I believe he would have done a hand stand and back flip with the slightest encouragement. So we did a little unpacking and I ordered a bottle of chardonnay and some snacks and two glasses but also an orange juice for the lady. On most cruises the dinner hour was one at 6:30 and the second at eight. She picked eight and wanted to rest and or nap a bit from the drive and excitement. The waiter arrived with a tray, set the contents, thanked me for the tip, and scurried away. I purred us a glass of wine with a small one for Meagan who would try it. We clinked glasses and I toasted our future. She took a sip and sat her glass down. She mentioned her folks didn't drink at home and so she really hadn't have any exposure to wine except at communion or a little that the ladies of her group would sneak from the hiding place. But that wasn't much. I finished my wine while she went to the couch to lay down. The suite had a large living room we are in with nicely decorated features, two couches and a table with chairs for eating, if one desires, the adjoining room was open at one end with king size bed and two baths and showers.

Meagan rose up from the nap as I was finishing my second glass of wine and the peanuts and cheese left on the tray. Since there was no big rush as our dinner reservations were for eight o'clock, we talked a little and she decided she ought to get dressed. I thought the same and retired to the men's area freshened up and put on a nice summer suit with open collar. We were soon ready and went down one flight and to our dinning room. The matradee met us and asked us for our table assignment and led us and seated the lady. We looked over the menu with it's usual provision for three entrees, meat, fish or vegetarian. There was one other couple sitting at our large table and we introduce ourselves, they where form New York and spoke very little. I ordered a glass of wine and Meagan lemonade. We finished with a disgustingly rich desert and had coffees in finishing. There was a stage show gong on but it was packed and we were late from dinner and so we went back to a lounge near our room and listened to a piano player with a bass. Nice, and it again made me think of my cocktail lounge jobs with the old college quintet. We were tired from a long day and bunking ride through choppy waters to our landing. So we readied for bed with nervous caution as it would ostensibly be her first with a man and I wasn't sure what to do but be slow and tender. She put on her special nightee and I pajamas although in truth I never wore them. The covers, when needed, were enough. She looked so pretty and I mentioned how beautiful she was and she smiled shyly. We got in the big king bed big enough for two couples at least and got close together me on the right side of her. We spoke softly of how happy we were and how great to be out of confinement and with a new lover and new life. We suddenly found ourselves like two youngsters playing footsie-footsie with a chuckle. We faced and kissed a nice long good night and shut down the lights.

I was as usual slow in getting to sleep but my partner was sound asleep. Morning came and we took a good look at one another and I said in jest. "Who are you? Are you in the wrong room". "No, she answered, I'm in a strange big bed with my new lover and I'm feeling happy as a cat although I don't know much about the habits of a cat". We laughed and made a good morning brighter. We dressed and went down to breakfast. We went out on the upper deck and sat facing the pool and the water slide. A waiter came by and I really wanted a Bloody Mary and asked Meagan what, if anything, she might like. She really never had a Bloody Mary and said she would taste mine but really wanted a cup of coffee. And so went the morning as we watched he parade of tourists, swimming, eating and up on the sun deck watching the harbor. Eventually we decided to eat at the buffet and not in the dinning room and got a real spread of salads, meats, cheese, fruits, and you can guess. After lunch we found the ice cream stand and poured out the half frozen chocolate in the cup. The afternoon found us up on the upper deck taking in the sun and napping. Since I had planned a surprise dinner dance at the same place we met and did the fatal dance, I suggested we pass on dinner on board and go to Charlie's 602 club for their dinner dance, I had made reservations. We showered, dressed with our finest and soon were ready to depart. We took a two seat ride behind the bicycle rider to the club. The head waiter wasn't the same as before but he seated us as promised at a table near the band. A waitress came with menus and took our drink order...a silver bullet for me....A small glass of zinfandel wine and a glass of water for the lady. She was so surprised at me remembering our meeting place and looked around the big room and spotted the large oval table on the far side where we first met and now look at us. When the head water passed by I called him over aliped him a twenty and asked him to have the band play our song 'Moonlight Serenade'. As we finishing our pre-prandial drinks, the waitress brought out our dinners. I again gather up my more formidable presence and asked lover to dance, she answered with the same churlish grin, "You are a devil, "I'd love to dance". I took her hand and led her to the floor as the band started playing my request. We danced closely and moved with the music as I planted a more firm kiss under the same ear and whispered "I love you even more than the first time and thank you for becoming my soon to be bride".

I could sense the tears slowly running down her cheeks, she softly spoke, "I'm so happy and I can' believe were at the place of the beginning of this love and I'm so happy you rescued me and we're out into the real world and be together for as long as we live". We danced some more and she even knew some moves with the faster jazzy tunes. Our food had gotten cold but we didn't care, we ordered the fanciest cake and ice cream along with a glass of champagne to celibate our new beginning. The band was about to finish for the evening as we left for our special suite and arrived with the same bicycle guy. We went immediately to undress and get ready for the big bed. We got into that bed again in the same positions and laid quietly very closely for a few minutes when suddenly she reached over with her right hand and took hold of me. I turned slightly toward her and reached my left hand over wrapping us together. I said softly "I love you so much" and she whispered back "I love you too even more." We were still quiet for a moment or two and over came her right leg (she had removed her night gown quickly as I did with my pants as we got in bed) as I felt her leg over me with my already growing member aroused. I turned her over on her back and moved with the turn and was on top of my waiting maiden. She reached out for me and we both met with four hands reaching for my now completely hard member and we moved it slowly into her sweet spot until it stopped. We moved together in a rhythm much like the rolling of the ship. She lifted her spread legs and wrapped them around my back and squeezed. Our motion together made the room seem like it was turning upside down.... Suddenly she gasped a bit and let go a slight scream and fell back while I made a corresponding grown in complete rapture. I'm thinking to myself and said out loud "We made it against many odds but now we're truly a complete pair'. I kissed her with heavy emotion and we just laid there clinched together. That calls for another Forsooth and a lowd one! The remainder of the night was quiet and we fell off and slept like babies. When we finally awakened we were still clinched together, looked at each, wondered if we had flown 'over-the-rainbow.' We had to hurry as the boat schedule showed departure at 8:45 for St Petersburg where we left the car. We made it with coffee, the big breakfast buffet style on board, found a table near the guard railing, and looked out over the deep blue water. I mentioned as we finished our breakfast that Disney World, Animal Kingdom, and Epcot Center were nearby and we could have a great time with all the exhibits, eating places and the old worn out retailers' saying 'and Much-much-more'.

She thought that would be great and had heard all about all the activates around Orlando Florida. And so we did. The car was okay and we headed for Orlando and a room for the night and then a tour of Epcot Center. In the morning we got some breakfast complementary at the motel and headed for the huge parking lot. We arrived, took a buggy ride to the entrance, paid for tickets, and entered the magic of Disney. You were first met with a tunnel enclosed in rail type cars whisking you along revealing the wonders of computerized advancement and Microsoft in it's infancy. The place a crowded and movement was slow. My favorite one was the Canadian exhibit. We took seats all of which were good as you have to look up to follow the presentation We walked around and I spotted the Swedish restaurant and suggested it for a late lunch. She okayed and we were seated. Some of the food specialties were fishy and very different from what Meagan got in the convent dinning room, but she tried the smaller displayed and liked some. We were a little tired and agreed we had seen enough and so we left and returned to our motel. I hadn't yet surprised her with the idea of a trip down to Florence to meet with Fr. Ray. He had sold out the horse farm to a new retired Priest and had a nice condo near the coast. He had invited me for any time to visit with notice as I had been there before. She thought that would be great and so we left early the next morning and drove on down. We arrived and were greeted by my friend, took us in, and showed us to a guest room. While, out of courtesy, he wouldn't comment, he really didn't know whether we were yet married or not. He was a great fumbling do-it-yourself cook and just had been shopping and had some fresh vegetables and shrimp.

I had packed some martini mixins' before I left on this trip along with a nice bottle of chardonnay and gave them to him for the evening cocktail hour. He started boiling the shrimp as we toasted our meeting once again. Might be the last time I'll ever see him again. We finished our drinks, meals and adjourned to the lanai for a chat. He wanted to know all about what happened since I talked with him for advice at about the time I was writing letters to Meagan at the Kentucky derby. So it was fairly obvious much had gone on since the talk about her stress treatment and dealing with the Convent. She joined the conversation and told of her nervous condition and the rehabilitation treatment and finally leaving the Convent without any punishment but becoming a lay person entitle to mass and right to take communion. I tuned in explaining my role in being responsible for doing my best after we discovered we were meant to be a pair and maybe permanent partners, and that was that. Father reminded us that it was he who listened to my requests for guidance when I confessed my love for this really institutionalized fair maiden. And now we are as happy as a couple of misguided clams. Although I suspect clams do not 'suffer the slings and arrows of the 'same' outrageous fortune' as do we mortals. We soon adjourned the conversation and got ready for bed as I reminded him we once sat up 'till the wee hours of the morning arguing whether one could honestly talk with the Lord. You insisted and played a tape with the young priest who apparently influenced you in thinking he could. I lost the debate or whatever you might call the heated raillery. However, we have had many opposing discussions and personify the truism that you don't have to agree with a person to leave a heated argument or a business deal and remain friends. I will make sure that will always remain true, having put to rest all of the admissions, confessions, questions answered and anything else, we three together held hands and kneeled down and silently prayed together...and time will tell. Anon.

Printed and bound by PG in the USA

USA2019PGIL